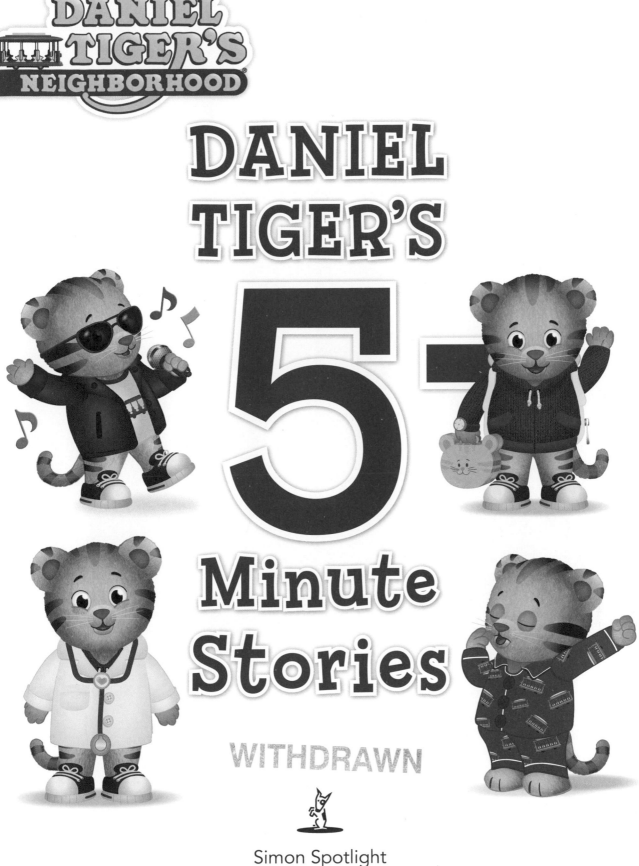

DANIEL TIGER'S NEIGHBORHOOD

DANIEL TIGER'S 5-Minute Stories

WITHDRAWN

Simon Spotlight

New York   London   Toronto   Sydney   New Delhi

SIMON SPOTLIGHT

An imprint of Simon & Schuster Children's Publishing Division
1230 Avenue of the Americas, New York, New York 10020

This Simon Spotlight edition May 2017

Daniel Goes to School, *Daniel Visits the Doctor*, and *Goodnight, Daniel Tiger* © 2014 The Fred Rogers Company

Daniel's First Sleepover, *Daniel's New Friend*, *Daniel Tries a New Food*, *The Baby Is Here!*, *Nighttime in the Neighborhood*, and *You Are Special, Daniel Tiger!* © 2015 The Fred Rogers Company

Daniel Goes to the Playground, *Daniel's First Fireworks*, and *Daniel's Winter Adventure* © 2016 The Fred Rogers Company

For information about special discounts for bulk purchases, please contact Simon & Schuster Special Sales at 1-866-506-1949 or business@simonandschuster.com.

Manufactured in China 1120 SCP

10

ISBN 978-1-4814-9220-1

ISBN 978-1-5344-0046-7 (eBook)

These titles were previously published individually by Simon Spotlight with slightly different text and art.

Contents

Goodnight, Daniel Tiger

It was a beautiful day in the neighborhood today, and now it is nighttime. Daniel Tiger needs to get ready for bed!

"Ding, ding, ding!" says Daniel, "Tigey wants to go for a trolley ride!"

Daniel wants to play, but . . . it's time to get ready for bed.

"I know you want to play," Mom says as she snuggles with Daniel, "but sleep is important so that you can grow. Do you remember what we do to get ready for bed?"

Daniel smiles and sings with Mom, *"Bathtime, pj's, brush teeth, story and song, and off to bed!"*

"Ding, ding! Hop aboard for a trolley ride to bathtime!"
Dad says.

Daniel laughs and takes a ride. "Ding, ding!"

Daniel wants to play, but . . . it's time to get ready for bed.

Daniel likes bathtime! As he scrubs, he plays and sings,
"Scrub, scrub, scrub my fur, up on top my head!
Scrubby-scrubby-scrubby-scrub, soon it's time for bed!"

Daniel imagines he is on a boat sailing the soapy seas. He sings, *"Sailing, sailing, sailing the soapy seas. Bring all your friends and come with me to sail the soapy seas!"*

Daniel wants to play, but . . . it's time to get ready for bed. Dad says, "You need to go to sleep at bedtime so that your great big imagination can rest."

"I do have a lot of imagining I want to do tomorrow!" Daniel says as Dad dries his fur.

Daniel sings, "Bathtime, pj's, brush teeth, story and song, and off to bed!" Daniel has taken his bath, and now it's time for his favorite trolley pj's.

"Next stop on the trolley ride is brush your teeth," says Dad. Daniel takes his toothbrush and hops up to the sink. Daniel sings, *"I gotta brusha, brusha, brush, brush my teeth at night if I want to keep them healthy and bright. I gotta brusha, brusha, brusha, brush my teeth!"* Daniel's teeth are all brushed!

"Let's take Tigey for a ride on Trolley," says Daniel. "Ding, ding, ding!"

Daniel wants to play, but . . . it's time to get ready for bed.

Mom holds Tigey up to her ear, "Oh, I see," she says to Tigey. Daniel stops playing and looks at Mom. What is she talking about with Tigey?

"Tigey wants to snuggle up in bed and hear a bedtime story," Mom explains.

Daniel snuggles up with Mom as she reads a bedtime story. Reading a story with Mom makes Daniel feel comfy and cozy. Daniel is sleepy. Daniel *does* want to go to bed.

Daniel quietly sings, *"Bathtime, pj's, brush teeth, story and song, and off to bed."* Then he yawns a big tired tiger yawn. Daniel does want to go to bed. Daniel is sleepy. "Mom and Dad, can you sing me my goodnight song?"

Mom and Dad sing, "Goodnight, Daniel, goodnight. It's time to go to sleep and when you awake, the sun will greet you with its bright and sunny face. Goodnight, Daniel, goodnight." Everyone in the neighborhood is going to sleep too.

Goodnight, Daniel Tiger, goodnight. And goodnight to YOU. Ugga Mugga!

Daniel Goes to School

"Hi, neighbor! It's time for school!" said Daniel Tiger.
"I've got my backpack. I've got my lunch box and . . ."
"You've got me!" said Dad, opening the front door.
"Now let's get you to school."

"Please take us to school, Trolley," said Daniel as he and Dad hopped aboard.

"*Ding! Ding!*" said Trolley.

"*We're going to school today. Won't you ride along with me? Ride along!*" sang Daniel.

When they arrived at school, Daniel pulled Dad into the classroom. "Come on, Dad. Let's go build with blocks!"
But Dad just stopped.

"I would love to build blocks with you," said Dad, "but I have to go to work."

"Are you sure?" Daniel asked. "Maybe work is closed today!"

Dad Tiger shook his head. "I don't think so, Daniel," he said. "It's time for me to go."

Daniel was sad. "I don't want you to go. I want you to stay and be with me."

"I want to stay too, Daniel," said Dad, "but all your friends are here, and Teacher Harriet will take good care of you. At the end of the day, I will come back and pick you up, because *grown-ups come back*."

"*Grown-ups come back,*" repeated Daniel. He gave Dad a hug good-bye. "Ugga Mugga."

"Ugga Mugga," said Dad.

Teacher Harriet gently led Daniel to the art table. "Let's see what your friends are doing."

Prince Wednesday was drawing a picture of his dad, King Friday. "My dad's at work being the boss of castle stuff," he said.

"My mom is at work too. I miss her," said Miss Elaina. "But look! I have her picture in my necklace to remind me that she'll come back to get me."

Daniel picked up a crayon. "I want to have a picture of my dad too. I'm going to draw us in a rocket ship, blasting off to the moon."

Daniel imagined that he and his dad really were blasting off to the moon. *Whoosh!*

"Come to the rug for circle time!" called Teacher Harriet, and everyone skipped over to the rug—everyone except Miss Elaina. Where was Miss Elaina?

Suddenly, Daniel heard "Oh no! Oh no! Oh no!" It was Miss Elaina.

"I can't find the picture of my mommy!" Miss Elaina sniffled. "If I don't have my picture, how do I know my mommy will come back and get me?"

Daniel put his arm around Miss Elaina. "Your mommy will come back and get you," he said. "My dad always says *'Grown-ups come back.'*"

"We can help you find your necklace," suggested Prince Wednesday. The whole class began to look.
They looked high.
They looked low.
They even looked backward. (Well, Miss Elaina did.)
Until . . .

"I found it!" hooted O the Owl, picking the necklace up off the ground.

"Thank you, O," said Miss Elaina happily.

"Owls are excellent lookers," said O the Owl.

"Owls are excellent friends, too," added Teacher Harriet.

Teacher Harriet looked at the clock. "We spent circle time looking for Miss Elaina's necklace," she said. "It's lunchtime now. Miss Elaina, would you like to be my lunch helper today?"

"Okay!" replied Miss Elaina.

At the table, Miss Elaina passed out the lunch boxes to her friends. As everyone munched on their food, there was a knock at the door. Who could it be?

It was the grown-ups! "All the grown-ups came back!" said Miss Elaina. She was so happy.

Daniel ran over to his dad. "You came back!"

"I did," replied Dad.

"Can we go build blocks now?" asked Daniel.

"I've been waiting all day!" Dad answered, smiling.

Daniel's New Friend

It was a beautiful day in the neighborhood, and Daniel and Miss Elaina went to Prince Wednesday's castle to play. "A royal welcome," said Queen Sara Saturday.

When Miss Elaina and Daniel got to Prince Wednesday's room,
they saw someone they didn't know.

"Hi, what's your name?" asked Miss Elaina.

"That's my cousin, Chrissie," said Prince Wednesday.

"Hi, Chrissie," said Daniel.

"It's nice to know you!" Chrissie smiled.

"We're playing knights!" said Prince Wednesday.

"I'll be the big knight!" said Miss Elaina, picking a knight up from the table.

"I'll be the silver knight!" said Daniel.

"And I'll be the flying knight!" said Chrissie, making her knight fly into the air. "Look out beloooooow!"

"Now let's dress up as knights!" said Prince Wednesday. "I have knight costumes."

"Grr-ific idea!" said Daniel.

Prince Wednesday asked his mom, Queen Sara Saturday, to help him find his knight costumes.

"Here they are!" Prince Wednesday exclaimed after he found the costumes in his dress-up trunk.

Daniel and Miss Elaina jumped up and ran over to Prince Wednesday to get a costume. But Chrissie didn't get up.

"Chrissie," called Daniel, "don't you want to play?"

"I'm coming," said Chrissie, "but I need my crutches to stand."

Queen Sara Saturday gave Chrissie her crutches, and Chrissie slowly stood up. Daniel could see she had something on her legs.

"What's on your legs?" he asked.

"My legs can't walk on their own," said Chrissie, "so the braces help me walk."

Daniel had never seen crutches or braces before.

"Can I touch your braces?" asked Daniel.

"Sure!" said Chrissie. "It won't hurt me!"

Daniel felt Chrissie's braces. They felt smooth and cool.

"Do you wear your braces all the time?" asked Miss Elaina.

"Not *all* of the time," replied Chrissie. "Not when I sleep, or take a bath. But most of the time . . . I even wear them to school!"

"You go to school?" asked Daniel. "We go to school too!"

"I'm just like you," said Chrissie, "but the way I walk is different."

"In some ways we are different, but in so many ways, we are the same," said Queen Sara Saturday. "You walk differently from each other, but you are the same in other ways. You all go to school, and you all like to play. We all have things about us that are the same, and things that are different."

Daniel thought about what Queen Sara Saturday said.
"So . . . do you like to play pretend?" he asked Chrissie.
"I love to play pretend!" Chrissie smiled. "It's my favorite, favorite!"
"Really?" exclaimed Daniel. "It's my favorite, favorite too!"
"You have the same favorite thing!" cheered Miss Elaina.
"So let's play!" exclaimed Prince Wednesday.

"*Roar!*" said Prince Wednesday. "I'm a dragon!"

"Careful! Don't bump Chrissie!" said Daniel.

"It's okay, Daniel. Sometimes I do need extra help," said Chrissie. "But I also like to do things by myself . . . just like you! And right now I'm Brave Knight Chrissie!"

"And I'm Brave Knight Daniel!" said Daniel, giggling. Daniel imagined that he was a brave flying knight, flying over a dragon to his castle.

"Come on, knights!" said Miss Elaina. "Let's stop that dragon!"

Daniel, Prince Wednesday, and Miss Elaina ran around Prince Wednesday's room. Around and around they went, until Daniel noticed . . . Chrissie was going slower than everyone else.

"Come on, Knight Chrissie!" exclaimed Daniel. "We have to go fast to catch the dragon!"

Chrissie shook her head. "I can't go as fast as you can."

"Oh no," said Daniel, "if you can't go as fast as us, then maybe we should stop playing!"

But Chrissie didn't want to stop playing. "I like being a knight!" she told Daniel. "I just need to play a different way."

"What do you mean?" asked Daniel.

"When you play knight, you run around. When I play knight, I stand and guard the castle!" Chrissie explained.

Daniel thought Chrissie really did look like a brave and bold guard for the castle.

"We can all be knights," he said. "Just different kinds of knights!"

"Not me!" said Prince Wednesday. "I'm a dragon!"

"Come on, knights!" said Daniel. "Let's stop that dragon!"

49

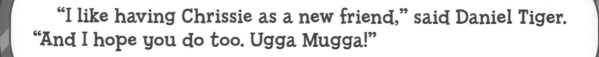

"I like having Chrissie as a new friend," said Daniel Tiger. "And I hope you do too. Ugga Mugga!"

50

Daniel Visits the Doctor

It was a beautiful day in the neighborhood, and Daniel was home, playing doctor.

"Okay, Tigey, it's time for Doctor Daniel to give you a checkup." Daniel giggled as he opened his toy doctor kit. Just then Mom Tiger came into the room.

"Oh hello, Doctor, have you seen my little tiger, Daniel?" Mom asked.

"Mom, it's me . . . Daniel! I'm not really a doctor!" Daniel giggled.

Mom smiled and ruffled Daniel's fur. "Well, Daniel, we have to get going. We're going to see Dr. Anna today for your checkup."

"But . . . Mom, I'm one stripe scared to go for a checkup," said Daniel. "What will happen there?"

Mom put her arm around Daniel and sang, *"When we do something new, let's talk about what we'll do."*

Mom showed Daniel what would happen at the doctor's office and started to draw. "The first thing that happens at the doctor is that you wait . . . in the waiting room." Daniel remembered that Dr. Anna's waiting room had a fish tank, books, and toys, too!

"The next thing that happens is that Dr. Anna will check your body to make sure it's healthy and strong. She'll check your heart—*thump, thump!* She'll check your ears—*tickle, tickle, tickle*— she'll check your eyes—*blink, blink*—and she'll check your throat— *aaaaaah!*"

Daniel took Mom's pictures to Dr. Anna's with him. "It's like a book!" said Daniel, as they headed out the door.

"It is like a book!" said Mom Tiger. "Let's see if you can find all the things we drew in our book . . . in Dr. Anna's office!"

"Okay!" said Daniel.

"Wow!" said Daniel as he looked around Dr. Anna's office. "The waiting room looks just like the picture we drew!" Daniel ran over to the fish tank. "Hi, fishies! *Blub, blub, blub!*"

"And now," said Mom, "we wait. *Wait, wait, wait in the waiting room.*"

While he was waiting in the waiting room, Daniel made-believe that the fish in the fish tank were going to see the doctor too!

"Daniel Tiger, and . . . Tigey Tiger," called Dr. Anna.
"It is time for your checkups. Follow me!"
Mom held Daniel's hand as they followed Dr. Anna.

Daniel climbed up on the table and looked around curiously. What was going to happen next?

Dr. Anna smiled and sang to Daniel, *"When we do something new, let's talk about what we'll do."*

First Dr. Anna listened to Tigey's heartbeat with a stethoscope. *"Thump, thump!"* Dr. Anna said with a smile.

Then Dr. Anna listened to Daniel's heartbeat. *Thump, thump!* "Your heart is strong and healthy, Daniel!" said Dr. Anna.

Dr. Anna even let Daniel listen to his own heart with the stethoscope! *Thump, thump!* Daniel thought that was so cool!

Dr. Anna used her otoscope to check Tigey's ears. *"Tickle, tickle, tickle!"* Dr. Anna said.

Then Dr. Anna checked Daniel's ears. *Tickle, tickle, tickle!* "The otoscope does tickle!" Daniel giggled.

61

Dr. Anna checked Daniel's eyes. *Blink, blink!*

And then she checked Daniel's throat. *Aaaaaah!*

Dr. Anna checked Tigey's height and weight. Tigey was a healthy weight and three stripes tall!

Then she checked Daniel's height and weight. Daniel was a healthy weight and eight stripes tall. "That's the perfect number of stripes for a tiger your age!" Dr. Anna said.

"Daniel and Tigey, you are both done with your checkups," said Dr. Anna, "and you both get a heart sticker for being such good patients."

"Grr-ific! Thanks, Dr. Anna!" said Daniel.

Back in the waiting room, Daniel saw his friend O the Owl.
"Hello, Daniel! I'm here for my checkup," said O, looking nervous.
"You are?" asked Daniel. "I just had my checkup!"
"What was it like?" asked O.
"You can read this book I made with my mom," said Daniel, handing O the book.
"A book?" said O happily. "I love books! Thanks, Daniel!"

Thanks for coming with me and Tigey to the doctor's office. Knowing what was going to happen helped me feel good about going to the doctor. And it might help you feel good too! Ugga Mugga!

Daniel Tries a New Food

It was a beautiful day in the neighborhood, and Daniel Tiger
and Tigey were going on an adventure . . . in the living room.

"Let's go in our cave!" said Daniel.

But when Daniel crept over to the cave, he saw that someone
was in there! Who was it?

It was Daniel's dad!

"Dad!" Daniel giggled. "What are you doing?"

"I'm not Dad! I'm . . . a silly beast!" said Dad.

"Well, I caught you, you silly beast!" said Daniel, hugging Dad tightly.

Daniel's mom came into the living room. "Daniel, my little adventurer," said Mom, "do you want to help me make something in the kitchen?"

Daniel jumped up happily. "Okay, Mom! I like being a big helper."

In the kitchen Daniel and Mom got ready to cook up a special treat.

"Since Miss Elaina is coming over for dinner tonight, I'm making a new dessert," said Mom. "It's called banana swirl!"

"Banana swirl?" asked Daniel. "What is that?"

"Well, I put these bananas in the freezer," Mom said.

"Brr!" said Daniel. "They're cold!"

"And now we put the bananas in the blender, put the top on, and press . . ."

"GO!" said Daniel, as he pushed the button with Mom.

The bananas swirled around and around in the blender.

"Okay, they're done!" said Mom, as she turned off the blender.

"Wow," said Daniel, "they don't look like bananas anymore."

Mom dipped a spoon into the banana swirl, and held it out to Daniel.

Daniel wasn't sure he wanted to try the banana swirl. "What if I don't like it?" he asked.

"It's true, you might not like it," said Mom. "But it might taste smushy yummy! Try a new food, it might taste good."

"Okay," said Daniel. "I'll try." And very slowly, he took a little bite and . . .

He liked it! "It's swirly, banana-y, it's cold and sweet, and it kind of tastes like banana ice cream!" said Daniel, grinning. "I like banana swirl!"

"I'm glad you tried it," said Mom.

Ding! Dong! The doorbell rang. "Miss Elaina's here!" exclaimed Daniel happily.

73

Daniel ran to the living room.

"Hiya, toots," said Miss Elaina.

"I'll call you when dinner is ready," Mom said from the kitchen.

Daniel and Miss Elaina went over to Daniel's cave.

"Let's pretend we're on an adventure," he whispered, "and we're looking for a silly beast!"

"I think I saw a silly beast over there in that cave!" exclaimed Miss Elaina. It's Tigey!

That gave Daniel an idea! He imagined that Tigey was a silly beast deep in the jungle.

"Dinnertime!" Dad called.

At the dinner table Mom was serving spaghetti, but it didn't have the regular tomato sauce on it.

"This is something new," said Mom as she scooped a big helping onto each plate. "It's called veggie spaghetti. These veggies go on top of the spaghetti."

Daniel looked closely at his plate. "I don't think I like veggie spaghetti," he said.

"But you've never tried veggie spaghetti," Mom said.

Daniel looked at the new food again. "That's true," he said. "I've never tried it." Daniel turned to Miss Elaina, who was about to take a bite. "What do you think?"

"Well, toots," said Miss Elaina, "at my house we always say *try a new food, it might taste good!*"

"We say that at my house too!" Daniel said, smiling.
And so Miss Elaina and Daniel both took a little bite and . . .

Daniel liked it! "It's crunchy and munchy!" Daniel said with a smile. "Veggie spaghetti is good!"

But what about Miss Elaina?

"It's not my favorite," said Miss Elaina, "but can I please have extra carrots? I love, love, love carrots!"

"Absolutely," said Mom Tiger. "I'm glad you both tried something new."

"Me too!" said Daniel as he ate more veggie spaghetti.

After they finished their dinner, it was time for the special dessert that Daniel and Mom had made together.

"Who wants banana swirl?" asked Mom.

"I do!" said Daniel.

"I do!" said Miss Elaina.

"Banana swirl?" said Dad. "But I've never had banana swirl before. What if I don't like it?"

"Try a new food, it might taste good!" said Daniel and Miss Elaina, giggling.

So Dad took a little bite and . . .

He liked it! "Banana swirl is smushy yummy," said Dad. "I'm glad I tried it."

"Me too!" said Daniel.

I liked trying banana swirl and veggie spaghetti at dinner. Have you ever tried a new food? Try a new food, it might taste good! Ugga Mugga!

Daniel's First Sleepover

It's nighttime in the Neighborhood of Make-Believe. Daniel Tiger is wearing his pajamas. But he's not going to bed just yet. . . .

Daniel is going to his first sleepover!

Daniel and Mom hop on Trolley to go to Prince Wednesday's castle.

Daniel is not sure what he's going to do at the sleepover. He sings, *"When we do something new, let's talk about what we'll do."*

Then Daniel asks Mom, "What will I do at the sleepover?"

Mom says, "You will do everything you do before going to bed at home. But you get to do it all with Prince Wednesday!" That sounds exciting to Daniel as he remembers all of the things he does before going to bed. Daniel brushes his teeth, reads a story, and sings a song.

Prince Wednesday is waiting for Daniel in his bedroom. "A royal hello to you!" says Prince Wednesday. "Boop-she-boop-she-boo! And to YOU too, neighbor!"

Daniel notices that they are both wearing their pajamas. Daniel has never worn his pajamas to someone else's house before! Daniel giggles and says, "Do you want to make believe with me? Let's make believe that we're having a pajama dance party!"

Daniel imagines that they are at a pajama dance party. All of Prince Wednesday's stuffed animals join the party too!

"Wasn't that grr-ific?" says Daniel. Daniel and Prince Wednesday are getting sleepy. It's dark outside in the Neighborhood of Make-Believe, and even the birds are going to sleep.

It's time for Prince Wednesday and Daniel to go to bed.

With lots of giggles and bubbles, Prince Wednesday and Daniel brush their teeth.

They even sing the same song when they brush their teeth!
"*I gotta brusha, brusha, brusha, brush my teeth at night if I wanna keep them healthy and bright. I gotta brusha, brusha, brusha, brush my teeth!*"

Brushing teeth together is something that makes sleepovers different and fun.

Now it's time for Daniel and Prince Wednesday to snuggle in bed to hear a bedtime story. They get cozy with lots of stuffed animal friends. Being together makes sleepovers different and fun!

King Friday reads the boys their favorite book, *Tigey, the Adventure Tiger*. King Friday is royally funny as he reads in all of the jungle animals' voices. The boys laugh and laugh.

Now it's time for a bedtime song. Daniel sings goodnight to Prince Wednesday. Prince Wednesday takes off his glasses and sings goodnight back to Daniel. Sleepovers make bedtime different and fun. Daniel smiles.

Now it's time to turn out the light and go to sleep. But wait!

There is a great big shadow on the wall. It looks scary to Daniel! What could it be? Daniel remembers, if something seems scary, *"See what it is, you might feel better."*

It's just Mr. Lizard! Mr. Lizard is not scary. Mr. Lizard is not scary at all!

Daniel hugs Mr. Lizard and crawls back into bed next to Prince Wednesday. Now they can go to sleep, together, at their very first sleepover.

Goodnight, Daniel. Goodnight, Prince Wednesday. And goodnight, neighbor. Ugga Mugga!

You Are Special, Daniel Tiger!

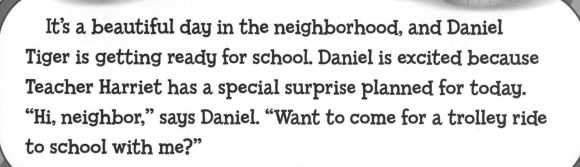

It's a beautiful day in the neighborhood, and Daniel Tiger is getting ready for school. Daniel is excited because Teacher Harriet has a special surprise planned for today. "Hi, neighbor," says Daniel. "Want to come for a trolley ride to school with me?"

Daniel loves Trolley. Daniel and Mom sing as they ride around the neighborhood to school, *"We're off to school today to play, learn, and sing. Won't you ride along with me? Ride along!"*

Daniel waves to his neighbors as he rides by. "Hi, Music Man Stan! Hi, Dr. Anna! Hi, Baker Aker! Hi, Mr. McFeely!"

"Hi, Daniel! Have a great day at school!" say the neighbors.

"Hello, Daniel Tiger!" says Teacher Harriet. "Come into the classroom and get ready for our special surprise!"

Daniel walks into school, puts his backpack in his cubby, and skips over to his friends. "This is going to be grr-ific," says Daniel.

Daniel and his friends don't have to wait very long to find out about the surprise. "Today we are going to put on a show!" explains Teacher Harriet. "Think of something special that you can do, and then stand on the stage and show it to your friends."

Prince Wednesday is first. The class chants, "Hi, Prince Wednesday. How do you do? Show us something special that you can do!"

Prince Wednesday exclaims, "I'm going to do a magic trick! Ready? Ta-da!" Prince Wednesday makes a rubber duck appear out of a hat.

Everyone cheers! Hurray for Prince Wednesday!

Katerina is up next. The class chants, *"Hi, Katerina. How do you do? Show us something special that you can do!"*

Katerina says, "Meow meow, I'm going to twirl!" Katerina twirls and leaps like a ballerina.

Everyone cheers! Hurray for Katerina!

O the Owl is sad. "I don't think I can do anything special, hoo hoo. I don't know any magic like Prince Wednesday and I can't twirl like Katerina," O tells Daniel.

Daniel tells his friend, "You are special, O the Owl." Then he sings, *"I like you, I like you, I like you just the way you are."*

107

It's Miss Elaina's turn. The class chants, *"Hi, Miss Elaina. How do you do? Show us something special that you can do!"*

Miss Elaina says, "This is my sheep puppet. Acting with puppets is my super-special talent." Miss Elaina acts out a silly play. The class loves her puppet show—it's so funny! Everyone cheers! Hurray for Miss Elaina!

108

It's Daniel's turn next. Daniel imagines himself putting on a big singing show with Tigey and all of his friends, singing and dancing as the audience cheers him on.

Daniel goes onstage. His friends chant, "Hi, Daniel Tiger. How do you do? Show us something special that you can do!"

Daniel says, "Singing makes me feel special. Here's my song: *My name is Daniel. Daniel Tiger. And I like to sing. La La La. My name is Daniel. Daniel Tiger. And I like my friends, just the way they are.*"

Everyone cheers. Hurray for Daniel!

It is O the Owl's turn next. But O the Owl doesn't want to go onstage. "Hoo hoo, I don't know what makes me special," O says sadly.

Daniel says, "O the Owl, you're smart and fun and you can read books and play the drums and do science experiments! You are special, O. And you are our friend."

Now O is smiling! "Thank you for helping me feel better," he says. "I think I know just what to do for my special talent."

The class chants, *"Hi, O the Owl. How do you do? Show us something special that you can do!"*

O takes a deep breath, and suddenly does the most fantastic flying flip only an owl can do! O takes a bow and says, "Flying is my special thing. I am special, just the way I am."

Everyone cheers. Hurray for O!

After the show, Dad comes to pick up Daniel from school. Daniel loves spending time just with Dad. Dad sings, "You are special to me. You are the only one like you, my friend. I like you. There's only one YOU in this wonderful world. You are special."

Daniel feels very special. He says, "I love you, Dad."

"I love you, too," Dad says.

The Baby Is Here!

It's a beautiful day in the neighborhood, and Daniel Tiger is very excited.

"Today is a special day," says Daniel. "Mom is going to have a baby!"

Everyone has lots to do to get ready for the new baby.
Daniel helps Mom and Dad get the baby's room ready.
"You can be a big helper in your family," Dad Tiger sings.
Daniel helps Dad paint the new baby's room.

Daniel helps Mom unpack his old baby clothes. Daniel can't believe he used to be little enough to wear this teeny-tiny sweater!

The baby's room is ready! But Daniel wants to do one more thing.

"The baby's room needs a picture of our family," Daniel says. First he draws a picture of himself. Next he draws the new baby. Then he adds Mom and Dad Tiger.

"Our family!" Daniel says.

Mom says, "It's time for Dad and me to go to Dr. Anna's office so she can help me have the baby."

Grandpere stays with Daniel while Mom and Dad go see the doctor.

While Daniel and Grandpere wait, Daniel tries to find something special he can give the new baby. He sees an old book at the bottom of his bookshelf called *Margaret's Music*. That was Daniel's favorite book when he was a baby! He thinks the new baby will like it too.

Finally, Mr. McFeely comes to tell Daniel that the new baby is here! Grr-ific! Grandpere and Daniel go to Dr. Anna's to visit Mom and Dad Tiger.

Dad Tiger greets Daniel and Grandpere at the door.
He takes Daniel in to see Mom Tiger.
Mom hugs Daniel and says, "I love you, Daniel Tiger!"
Daniel hugs her back and says, "I love you!"

Mom asks, "Do you want to meet your baby sister?"
Daniel nods excitedly.

Daniel is so happy to meet his new sister. He smiles at
the baby. She has the cutest little baby nose and the
sweetest little baby ears!

"Hi, baby sister. I'm your big brother, Daniel," he says. The baby looks right at Daniel and puts her paw on his paw.

Daniel says that he brought a special present for the baby. He takes out the *Margaret's Music* book.

"Margaret is a lovely name," says Mom.

Grandpere agrees. "It was my mother's name."

"Are you thinking what I'm thinking?" Dad asks. "Margaret is a perfect name for our baby!"

Hurray! Daniel helped name his baby sister.

125

Daniel wants to give Margaret the book, but the baby starts to cry.

"Why is Margaret crying?" Daniel asks Mom.

"Maybe she's hungry," says Mom. "I'm going to feed her."

Daniel decides to give his present to Margaret later.

It's time to take Baby Margaret home in her stroller. Daniel helps Mom push her through the neighborhood and introduce her to all the neighbors.

"She's so sweet!" says Baker Aker.

"She is music to my ears!" says Music Man Stan.

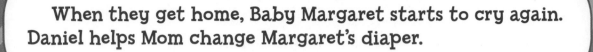

When they get home, Baby Margaret starts to cry again. Daniel helps Mom change Margaret's diaper.

Daniel wants to help make Baby Margaret feel better. He shows her the book *Margaret's Music*.

Baby Margaret stops crying! Daniel is proud to be a big brother—and a big helper.

Margaret played piano at the playground, and it sounded like Plink Plink Plink!

Ugga Mugga from Margaret and me to you!

Daniel Goes to the Playground

It was a beautiful day in the neighborhood, and Daniel and his family were at the playground with Prince Wednesday and Miss Elaina.

"Hi, neighbor!" said Daniel. "Margaret and I are swinging. One day she'll be big enough to go on a big kid swing like me! Right, Margaret?"

"Dan-Dan!" said Baby Margaret as she watched Daniel.

After swinging, Daniel and his friends decided to play circus. Daniel's mom and dad sat down nearby to watch the show with Baby Margaret.

First, Prince Wednesday swung on the flying trapeze.

Next, Miss Elaina walked the tightrope forward . . .

. . . and backward!

Then it was Daniel's turn. Daniel was going to juggle.

"And now, Daniel Tiger the Grr-ific will do his tigertastic juggling act!" said Daniel proudly. Daniel threw one, two, three juggling balls up in the air!

"Mom! Dad! Look at me!" Daniel exclaimed as he tried to catch the balls.

But Daniel's mom and dad weren't looking at Daniel. . . . They were helping Margaret.

133

Daniel was sad. "You didn't see me juggling," he said to his mom and dad.

"I'm sorry, Daniel," said Mom. "Your sister needed us."

"But I needed you too," said Daniel.

"I know it can be hard when we need to pay attention to Margaret," said Mom.

"It is hard," said Daniel. "Before Margaret, you used to watch me all the time."

"It is different with Margaret around," said Mom. "But *when a baby makes things different, find a way to make things fun.*"

Daniel tried to think of a way that Margaret could make things more fun. He thought and he thought until . . .

Margaret toddled over to Daniel, rolling the juggling balls toward him.

"That gives me an idea!" Daniel exclaimed. "Baby Margaret can help me with my juggling act, and then everyone can watch *both* of us! That will be lots of fun."

"Ga, ga, ga," said Margaret.

"Presenting Daniel the Grr-ific and his sister, Margaret the Magnificent!" announced Daniel.

Daniel tossed a ball to Margaret, and Margaret rolled it back to him. They were juggling *together*! And this time, everyone was watching.

Playing circus on the playground was so much fun, Daniel made-believe that he was performing in a real circus.

"It's time for the circus parade!" announced Miss Elaina. "Everyone, line up!"

Daniel, Prince Wednesday, and Miss Elaina all got in a line.

Margaret got in line too.

"No-no, Margaret, this parade is just for big kids," said Daniel.

Daniel and his friends paraded around the swings and the sandbox. But everywhere they went, Margaret went too!

"Mom!" said Daniel. "Margaret is too little to be in the parade."

"Hmm," said Mom. "Can we make room for everyone in the parade, even little tigers?"

"That would be different," said Daniel.

"It will be different, but *when a baby makes things different, find a way to make things fun*," Mom reminded Daniel.

Daniel looked over at Margaret, and she made a silly face. Daniel giggled. "Margaret, you are so silly!" Just then Daniel got another grr-ific idea!

"Maybe . . . Margaret can be the clown in our parade. That would be different and fun," said Daniel.

"Booboobooboo," said Margaret.

"Let the parade begin . . . again!" said Daniel happily.
And they all paraded around the playground together.

"I loved playing at the playground today with Margaret," said Daniel. "Do you have a baby in your family? How do you feel when things are different? It's different for me with Baby Margaret. But now I know that different can be fun! Ugga Mugga!"

Daniel's First Fireworks

It was almost nighttime in the Neighborhood of Make-Believe, and Daniel and his family were having a picnic dinner in the backyard so they could see the fireworks. Daniel had never seen fireworks before.

Daniel brought a picnic basket over to the blanket and sat down next to Mom.

"What's in the picnic basket?" asked Mom Tiger.

"Picnic stuff," said Daniel. "Like plates, cups, napkins, food, and . . . Tigey!" Daniel pulled Tigey out of the picnic basket and hugged him close. "Tigey wants to see the fireworks too."

"Well, it's not quite time for dinner or fireworks," said Mom. "Why don't you and Margaret play?"
"Okay!" said Daniel. "Come on, Margaret!"

"Come back here!" Daniel called out as a giggling Margaret toddled around the backyard.

Daniel and Margaret were having so much fun, they didn't even notice that it was getting darker. Until suddenly they saw something new floating around them.

"Look, Margaret! Fireflies!" Daniel exclaimed, pointing to the little flickering lights. "Let's say hi!"

But Margaret didn't want to say hi to the fireflies.
Margaret didn't know what they were.

"Margaret, come back!" said Daniel as Margaret toddled to Mom. "The fireflies are nice. They won't hurt you!"
Daniel followed Margaret back to the picnic blanket.

"Why doesn't Margaret like the fireflies?" he asked Mom.

"Well, Margaret has never seen a firefly before. To her, they're new. And new things can be scary sometimes."

"Can I help her?" asked Daniel.

"Yes, I think you can," said Mom. *"When something is new, holding a hand can help you."*

"When something is new, holding a hand can help you," sang Daniel as he took Margaret's hand. "Come on, Margaret. I'll hold your hand, and we can look at the fireflies together."

Daniel and Margaret held hands and walked back to the fireflies.

"Look at how the fireflies light up," said Daniel. "It's like they're twinkling and saying hi!"

Margaret looked at Daniel, and she looked at the fireflies. "Hi! Hi!" She giggled.

"Margaret isn't as scared anymore!" said Daniel happily.

Watching the fireflies gave Daniel an idea. Daniel imagined that he was a firefly, dancing with his firefly friends.

"Daniel, Margaret!" called Mom. "Come over to the picnic blanket for dinner."

Daniel helped take Margaret to the blanket, where Dad was serving sandwiches, carrots, and grapes.

"Mmm . . . picnic food is tigertastic!" said Daniel.

"It does taste better outside, doesn't it?" said Dad.

Suddenly, Daniel heard a loud noise. *Boom! Boom! Boom!*
"What is that noise?" asked Daniel. He was scared.
"Those are fireworks," said Dad. "See? Up in the sky!"
"Look how pretty they are," said Mom. "They're kind of like fireflies."
"But . . . they're really loud," said Daniel nervously.
"Fireworks are loud," said Dad, "but that's just the noise they make."

All of a sudden Daniel felt a small hand holding his. It was Margaret.

"Fireworks are new for you *and* Margaret. Maybe you can help each other," said Mom.

"*When something is new, holding a hand can help you,*" Daniel sang as he squeezed Margaret's hand.

"Come on, my fuzzy guy," said Dad. "Hold my hand too, and let's go get a better look at the fireworks."

"Okay," said Daniel. "But . . . I want to keep holding Margaret's hand too."

Boom! Boom! Boom! The fireworks were very loud.

But Daniel squeezed Margaret's hand. And Margaret squeezed Daniel's hand right back.

Daniel, Margaret, Mom, and Dad watched as the fireworks lit up the sky with sparkly, bright colors. And Daniel and Margaret liked them!

"Sometimes new things can be scary. But just remember, when something is new, holding a hand can help you. Ugga Mugga!"

Daniel's Winter Adventure

It was a snowy day in the neighborhood, and Daniel and Prince Wednesday were playing outside.

"Snowball catch!" said Daniel as he tossed a snowball to Prince Wednesday.

"Got it!" said Prince Wednesday, giggling as the snowball landed on his head. "Sort of."

Just then Daniel's dad came over, holding ice skates and pulling Daniel's sled behind him.

"The pond is frozen and safe for ice-skating," said Dad. "Are you two ready to go?"

"Yes!" said Daniel and Prince Wednesday.

"Okay, hop on the sled," said Dad. "Next stop, the ice-skating pond!"

"Yay!" cheered Daniel and Prince Wednesday.

"The skating pond is just down that hill," said Dad.

"That *BIG* hill?" asked Daniel.

"That royally big hill?" added Prince Wednesday.

"I—I don't think I can sled down that hill," said Daniel. "What if we go too fast? Or tip over? I can't do it. It's too hard."

"If something seems hard to do, try it a little bit at a time," sang Dad.

"But how do we sled down a big hill a little bit at a time?" asked Daniel.

"If we walk down the hill, closer to the bottom, you can sled down a little bit of the big hill," said Dad.

Together they walked down the hill. "Hey!" Daniel said. "From down here it doesn't look so hard! I think I can do it."

So they sledded down a little bit of the hill, and it wasn't hard at all—it was fun!

"Hmm," Daniel began, looking back at the sledding hill. "Maybe we could go a bit higher?"

"A royal yes!" exclaimed Prince Wednesday.

They sledded down the hill from a little higher up, and it was even more fun!

"Ready to sled down the big hill?" Prince Wednesday asked Daniel.

"I'm ready!" said Daniel.

"One . . . two . . . three . . . GO!" Daniel and Prince Wednesday shouted.

Daniel loved sledding down the big hill so much that he imagined he was on a superfast racing sled.

When Daniel, Dad, and Prince Wednesday arrived at the skating pond, they saw Miss Elaina and her mom, Lady Elaine. "Look!" said Daniel, "It's Miss Elaina . . . and she's ice-skating!"

"Hi, Dani—*OOF!*" said Miss Elaina as she fell down.
"Ice-skating is a little . . . whoa—oh—oh—slippery! But I like it."
"It looks . . . hard," said Daniel softly.

Dad called Daniel over to a bench to put on his ice skates.

"Dad?" said Daniel. "I'm not sure I want to go ice-skating anymore. . . . What if I fall?"

"Daniel," said Dad, "do you remember what to do when something seems hard?"

Daniel nodded. *"If something seems hard to do—like ice-skating—try it a little bit at a time."*

Dad helped Daniel try skating a little bit at a time.

First Daniel took
Dad's hands . . .

then he bent his
knees and looked
straight ahead . . .

and marched his feet:
March! March! March!

Until finally:
"I'm skating! I'm skating!"
said Daniel happily.

"*Oof!* I fell," said Daniel. "But I'm okay! And I'm ready to try again."

Just as Daniel skated back to the bench, Mom Tiger arrived at the pond with Daniel's baby sister, Margaret.

Margaret stepped one foot toward Daniel.

"Look, Daniel!" Mom said. "I think Margaret wants to try to walk for the first time!"

"Come on, Margaret! You can do it!" said Daniel. "Just try it a little bit at a time."

Margaret took one step . . . and another . . . and another . . . until she walked all the way over to Daniel!

"Margaret, you did it!" cheered Daniel. "You walked! I tried something new today, and you did too."

Daniel was so happy to try sled riding and ice-skating today, even if they seemed hard at first.

Is there something new that you would like to try? Just remember, *if something seems hard to do, try it a little bit at a time.* Ugga Mugga!

Nighttime
in the Neighborhood

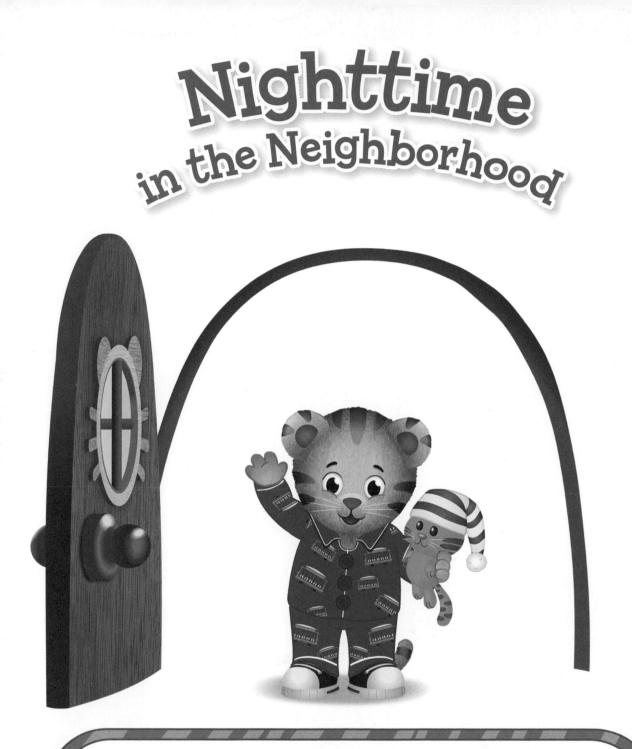

It was almost nighttime in the Neighborhood of Make-Believe, but Daniel Tiger wasn't going to bed. Something special was happening: Daniel was going to a special storytime at the library . . . at night! He had been waiting all day, and now it was finally time to go to the library.

"Look how beautiful the sky is," said Mom Tiger.

"It is grr-ific," said Daniel. "But . . . why is it so many different colors?"

"Well, the sky changes colors when the sun goes down. Day is turning into night," said Dad Tiger.

Daniel looked up into the night sky. "Look at all the stars," he whispered.

"I think we should walk to the library," said Mom Tiger, "so we can see all the things that are special at night."

"Tigertastic. *Let's find out what's special at night,*" said Daniel.

"*It's a beautiful night in the neighborhood,*" sang Daniel and his family as they walked to the library.

As Daniel walked through the neighborhood he heard many different sounds.

In the grass Daniel heard: *ribbit, ribbit, ribbit.*

It was a frog!

Up in a tree Daniel heard: *tweet, tweet, tweet.*

It was a nightingale!

On the ground Daniel heard: *chirp, chirp, chirp.*

It was crickets.

"There are so many different noises at night," said Daniel.

The Tiger Family walked down Main Street.

"Everything is so dark," said Daniel. "All the lights are out at Music Man Stan's Music Shop."

"Most of the shops are closed at night," said Mom.

"Look!" Daniel gasped. "I see a light in the bakery!"

Daniel peered in the window of the bakery and saw Baker Aker.

"What is Baker Aker doing?" Daniel asked.

"He's making bread so it will be fresh for the neighbors tomorrow," said Dad.

"Oh," said Daniel. "I didn't know he did that. Goodnight, Baker Aker."

The Tiger Family kept walking toward the library in the calm, cool night.

"Look, Daniel," said Mom. "The fireflies are out."

Daniel saw a group of fireflies flying around.

"Margaret and I will play with you, fireflies!" Daniel giggled.

Daniel looked up at the sky. "There are so many stars, but I only see them at night. Where are they during the day?"

"They are always there," said Dad, "but we can only see them when it's dark."

"I like looking at the stars," said Daniel.

"Me too," said Dad. "I like to look for pictures in the stars. Like . . . those stars look like a bear. But you have to use your imagination to see it."

When Daniel used his imagination, he could see the pictures in the stars. Daniel made believe that he was playing with the stars in the sky.

At last the Tiger Family arrived at the library. "We're here!" exclaimed Daniel. "It's time for the pajama party!"

When Daniel walked into the library, he saw his friends.

"Hi, toots!" said Miss Elaina. "I'm wearing my pajamas in the library!"

"Me too!" giggled Daniel.

"Me three!" said Prince Wednesday.

"Hoo hoo. Tonight we're going to do everything in our pajamas," said O the Owl.

And that is exactly what they did.

First they sang a song and danced in their pajamas.

Then they played a game in their pajamas.

Finally they listened to a story in their pajamas.

When the story was over, it was time for everyone to go home and go to bed.

"But . . . I'm not sleepy!" said Miss Elaina. But then she yawned. "Okay, maybe I'm a little sleepy."

"Don't fall asleep yet," said Music Man Stan. "You don't want to miss a nighttime ride on Trolley."

Ding! Ding! Trolley rolled through the Neighborhood of Make-Believe, taking each of the neighbors home to their beds.

Thanks for coming to the library with me tonight. I liked being out at night. Did you? Goodnight, neighbor. Ugga Mugga!